They're Coming For You 2

More Scary Stories that Scream to be Read

Other BOOks by
O. Penn-Coughin

They're Coming For You
Scary Stories that Scream to be Read

They're Coming For You 3
Scary Stories that Scream to be Read... Thrice*

They're Coming For You 4
Scary Stories that Scream to be Read... Forthwith*

They're Coming For You
Box Set, Vol. 1-3
Scary Stories that Scream to be Read*

They're Coming For You
Deluxe Coffin Box Set, Vol. 1-4
Scary Stories that Scream to be Read*

They're Coming For You
Scary Stories that Scream to be Read
Bloody Valentine Edition*

Vampire Ghost:
Book One: The Short Life and Many Deaths
of Harry "Dead Baby" Wilson*

* Now available in eBook format
coming soon in paperback

Listen to O. Penn-Coughin on The Scary Story Podcast

They're Coming For You 2
More Scary Stories that Scream to be Read

You Come Too
Publishing

O. Penn-Coughin

They're Coming For You 2 *More Scary Stories that Scream to be Read*
Published by You Come Too Publishing, Bend, Oregon.

Text copyright © 2010 by O. Penn-Coughin.
Illustrations copyright © 2010 by O. Penn-Coughin.

Cover art and illustrations by O. Penn-Coughin

Printed in the United States of America
First edition, 2010
Second edition, 2011

ISBN-13: 978-1463607166
ISBN-10: 1463607164

For Toad and Mag,
my two favorite children in the whole world

Tombstone
of Contents

Introduction

There are two types of people: scary story people and the other kind. I'm glad you are the first kind. But if you're not, it's not too late. There's still time to join us—or to put down this book.

Scary story people are usually also roller coaster people. If you love one, you almost have to love the other. (I'm an exception to this rule. I love scary stories but am terrified even of Ferris wheels. *Especially* of Ferris wheels. Go figure.) Reading or listening to a scary story is very much like taking a roller coaster ride in the safety of your own mind. Sometimes both can make you shut your eyes, laugh, scream, or even throw up. By the way, throwing up in your own mind is not as bad as it sounds. Your stomach doesn't hold grudges and the clean up's a breeze.

These stories are meant to be enjoyed out loud or alone if—as they say—you dare. Either way, the whole point is to have fun. I had a lot fun writing these stories. I hope you have fun reading them.

So strap in, hold on tight, and enjoy the ride!

O. Penn-Coughin

Death of a Ghost Hunter

"Tonight on *Ghost Stalkers* we investigate the chilling case of Moore Elementary School, which is said to be haunted," Matt Matherson said looking into the lens. "The school has been closed for more than 50 years, but the stories—and the ghosts—refuse to die."

The green glow of the night vision camera cast an eerie light over everything and whited out Matt's eyes.

"It all happened here, back in the last century," Esther Wilmington said, walking down the hall. "Over the years, eight children died in Room 6 under mysterious circumstances. According to rumors—never proved—those kids literally died of boredom. These rumors—again, never proved—claim that the teacher put her students to sleep with her lessons. And that, sadly, some never woke up."

"Later, the authorities found that the true cause of the deaths was a gas leak," Jerry Harrison said. "According to survivors, old Mrs. Bonyhady's part in it was that she always had the heat turned way up and kept the windows tightly shut."

"As a precaution, we are all equipped with our own gas detectors and emergency oxygen tanks tonight," Matt said. "Still, I hope you keep that bean burrito you had for dinner to yourself, Jerry."

They all laughed and walked into Room 6.

"There are some old timers who refuse to believe the science, though," Esther said. "They still maintain that it was Mrs. Bonyhady's boring lessons that killed those kids."

"Aaaaaaaaaah," the cameraman yawned suddenly, trying to sound like a dead child. "I'm sooooooo sleeeeeepy."

It was what the director called a "fakeout." During the entire history of the show they had never come across any real ghosts, so the cast and crew would make things up from time to time to keep the viewers interested.

"What the blank was that?" Jerry said into the camera, his eyes growing large. "I have a blank feeling about this blank."

(The bleeps would be added later. Everyone agreed that the fake swearing made the show seem more real.)

"I don't know!" Esther shouted.

They became quiet and looked around, waiting.

Nothing happened.

"Gas readings appear normal," Jerry said.

The camera showed the empty desks and some overturned chairs. An ancient green chalkboard covered one entire wall. Broken glass littered the floor by the narrow, tall windows.

"What a terrible place to die," Esther said, shaking her head.

"Let's get out of here," Jerry said.

"You two keep exploring the first floor," Matt said as they stepped back out into the hall. "I'll take a look down in the basement."

In reality, Matt was headed up to the second floor, where he was supposed to put on a ghost costume and pop out of the girls' bathroom.

"Will do," Jerry said.

The camera followed Jerry and Esther as they walked down the long, dark corridor. Suddenly, a shadow crossed in front of them and disappeared into one of the rooms.

A rush of fear and excitement passed through Esther.

"Let's follow it," she said.

"Huh?" Jerry said. "Oh, right."

Inside the dark room, their headlamps illuminated the desks and chairs.

"Nothing out of the ordinary here," Jerry said.

Then they heard the sobbing. Esther pointed a shaky finger at the corner where a little girl sat with her back to them. She was holding her head in her hands.

"Help, help, help," she whispered. "Help him."

Horror-struck, the two ghost hunters said nothing.

"Class has started," the girl said, fading as she turned toward them. "And he won't be able to stay awake for long."

She then disappeared down into the floor. Jerry and Esther ran out to the hall.

"None of that was in the script, man!" Jerry said nervously. "I'm getting out of here."

"Not without Matt," Esther said.

They hurried up the stairs to the girls' bathroom. The cameraman followed.

Back in Room 6, Matt sat down at one of the desks. There was a dusty, old book in front of him.

"Hey, I don't remember this being here before," he said yawning.

"Class, we have a new student joining us today," an old voice said. "Please turn to page 247."

Even though the windows were broken, it was suddenly very warm in the room. The gas detector was still normal. Several ghost children now sat at the other desks, their heads down. Matt could hear some of them snoring, but he was strangely untroubled. His eyelids grew heavy.

"George Washington was the father of our country. He chopped down that cherry tree, children, and could not tell a lie..."

"Stay awake, Matt!" Esther shouted somewhere upstairs. "Whatever you do, do not fall asleep!"

"Shhh, keep it down," Matt slurred as he slumped down in his little chair. "Some of us are trying to *zzztudeee*..."

"Find the verb in this sentence. Spell the word *misspell*," the teacher continued. "Forty-eight divided by six equals..."

By the time they found him, it was too late. Matt was face down in a pool of his own drool.

"Good," Mrs. Bonyhady said, blocking the door. "More new students."

Missing Cat

"Five. Hundred. Dollars." Morgan kept repeating each word slowly. "Five. Hundred. Dollars."

He stood in front of the telephone pole staring at a flyer. The photo showed a longhaired white cat being held by an old woman with thick glasses. The generous reward was being offered for *Mister Framboise*.

"That's such a lame name for a cat," Morgan said to the poster. "Well, Mister Framboise, I'm gonna find you anyway."

Morgan saw a lot of cats that week, but not the one he was looking for.

He felt the $500 slipping away. Then he got an idea. He would paint one of those other cats to look like Mister Framboise.

"That stupid, old woman is probably half-blind," Morgan muttered. "She won't be able to tell the difference."

It didn't take Morgan long to find a longhaired black cat that looked to be the right size. Then he bought some hair dye at the drug store.

"Just hold still, Mister Framboise," Morgan shouted.

After some awful meowing, hissing, and scratching, Morgan had his white cat. It wasn't perfect—a few black spots still showed here and there—but it was good enough to get the job done.

Morgan called the number on the flyer.

"I think I found your cat," he said into the phone.

"Oh, that's wonderful," the old voice said. "Can you bring him over after the sun goes down?"

"Sure," Morgan said. "No problem."

After dinner, Morgan put the white cat in a cardboard box and walked over to the house. He rang the doorbell. The old woman from the picture opened the door.

"Here's your cat," Morgan said.

"Oh, my," the woman said, opening the box. "Mister Framboise, there you are. I was beginning to think I would never see you again. Please come in, young man."

The cat jumped out of the box and ran down the sidewalk.

It was dark in the living room, the only light coming from a few candles. Dust and cobwebs covered everything. The old woman brought Morgan some cookies and milk.

These are actually pretty good, Morgan thought, finishing the last one. *But this milk tastes nasty.*

"That's because I put a little something in it to help you relax," the old woman said without moving her lips. "And to help get the blood flowing."

"What? Hey, how did you know what I was thinking?" Morgan slurred, the room starting to spin. "Where's my money anyway? I brought, I brought, I brought back your cat."

"Oh, that's not my cat," the woman said.

"How could you tell?" he asked, his tongue growing too thick to speak. "You only *thaw, thaw, thaw* him for a *th-th-th*-second."

"I don't have a cat," she said.

Morgan tried to get up from the chair, but his legs didn't work. He tried to scream. But he was powerless.

The old woman came toward him. He could smell the death on her as she leaned in close. She then opened her mouth and her dentures dropped down into Morgan's lap. He saw the sharp fangs poke out from her pink-black gums. A second later they dug deep into his neck.

As the life drained out of him, the last thing Morgan saw was the old woman changing, becoming younger and more beautiful with every drop. With every precious drop...

El Chupacabras

Somewhere near the border between Arizona and Mexico, the three friends sat around the campfire. It had been a long day. In the distance a storm was gathering strength.

"My feet hurt," Duncan said.

"Tell me about it," Whitney said, throwing another branch on the fire.

"My shoulders are killing me," Jeremy said. "That backpack weighs a—"

There was a rustling in the nearby bushes.

"What was that?" Whitney said.

Suddenly a dog-like creature ran toward them. It stopped, gave a crazy-eyed stare, and howled. Then it jumped through the fire and back into the darkness.

"Man, that was nuts," Duncan said.

"I thought animals were supposed to be naturally afraid of fire," Jeremy said.

"Seemed like something spooked that coyote real bad," Whitney said. "Real bad."

A streak of lightning lit up the nearby saguaros. Thunder rumbled overhead. A cold wind began to blow. The storm was getting closer.

Just then an old man stumbled into camp. His hair was white and a tattered poncho covered his frail body. Thick wrinkles crisscrossed his leathery face. The old man's little eyes were filled with fear and he was out of breath. He sat down without waiting for an invitation.

"What are you doing out here?" Jeremy asked. "Are you lost?"

"*El Chupacabras viene por mi, El Chupacabras viene por ti,*" the old man whispered, shivering.

"What's he talkin' about?" Whitney said.

"English, please," Duncan said.

Everyone was quiet for a while and then the old man spoke again.

"*El Chupacabras viene por mi, El Chupacabras viene por ti.*"

"What's he sayin'?" Whitney asked in a high-pitched voice.

"You should have learnt you some Spanish," Jeremy said.

"You should have learnt *you* some Spanish," Whitney said.

The fire danced in the old man's beady eyes and rain began to fall. Thunder and lightning closed in all around. The wind spit sand into their faces.

"This is starting to creep me out," Duncan said, putting on his jacket.

The old man wrapped his poncho tighter around himself and just repeated, "*El Chupacabras viene por mi, El Chupacabras viene por ti.*"

"I wish you would just shut up!" Whitney shouted. "You keep sayin' that and we done told you, we can't understand what it means."

The wind howled louder and the old man answered.

"*El Chupacabras viene por mi, El Chupacabras viene por ti.*"

As lightning flashed overhead, the old man suddenly jumped up and threw off his poncho. He started shaking

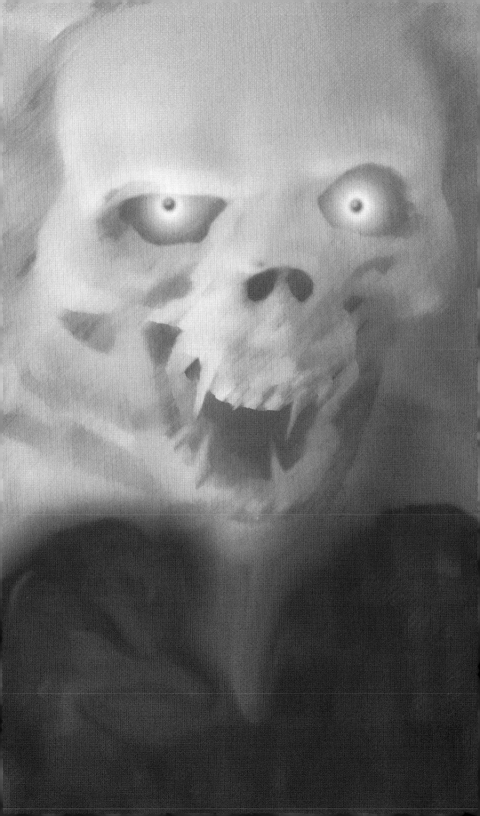

and circling the fire in a kind of insane dance. Slowly at first, and then faster and faster.

"Now what's he doing?" Whitney said, his eyes looking like the coyote's.

The old man kept dancing and shouting.

"*¡El Chupacabras viene por mi! ¡El Chupacabras viene por ti!*"

The last thing they saw was the old man lunge toward them with the speed of a wild animal.

The last thing they heard was the *thing*—no longer an old man—saying, "*El Chupacabras viene por mi, El Chupacabras viene por...AAAAAH!*"

Before turning into a blood-thirsty beast, the old man kept repeating, "The goat sucker is coming for me, the goat sucker is coming for... AAAAAH!

Red Barn

There was something wrong with the red barn. Mary had felt it the first day her family moved into the large house on 10 acres in the country. The barn was the first thing she saw as the moving truck pulled up, and she felt the wrongness of it deep down inside.

It was old and had been left out in the rain too long, mold covering as much of it as the fading, red paint. But it wasn't the exterior that troubled Mary. There was something in its bones that wasn't right, something that could not be explained away as just a bad case of the creeps.

Mary stayed as far away from it as possible.

And then came the winter.

Even in summer the house had been chilly for most of the day, but now it was downright cold around the clock. The old heating system couldn't keep up with the dropping temperature.

"We can't go on like this," Mary's mom said one night in December. "It's freezing in here."

When Mary got home from school the next day, she saw her father swinging an ax in front of a large pile of wood outside the red barn.

"I repaired that old wood stove today," he said as he brought the ax down. "Could use your help stacking this in the barn, Mare."

Mary felt her heart start playing hopscotch inside her chest at the thought of going into the old barn. But she reminded herself that her father was right there, a few feet away. What could happen?

She got some gloves from the house and began picking up pieces of splintered wood. She focused on the work and the sound of the ax outside, trying not to think about where she was.

"This isn't so bad," she told herself as she got into the rhythm of her task.

But every once in a while, it hit her. The dark evil of the place was there, all around her. Waiting. Waiting.

It was cold in the barn, cold enough that she could see her breath, but by the time she finished Mary was hot and sweaty.

She let out a long sigh.

"All done, Dad."

That night the house was nice and warm. Everyone was in a good mood.

Mary was filled with relief at having the wood stacking behind her. There'd be no reason now for her to have to go back inside the barn for a long time, and that made her happy.

But a few nights later, all that changed.

"My back's killing me, Mare," her dad said. "You think you could bring in some wood from the barn?"

Mary shuddered at the thought of going down to that sinister barn at this hour of the night. She slowly pulled on her boots and gloves.

It was cold and clear outside, but Mary didn't look up at the stars. She kept her head down, focusing on the small bit of ground illuminated by her flashlight. She could feel the barn out there, watching and waiting. Waiting for her.

It took all of Mary's courage to open the heavy, wooden door and step inside. It was even colder in the barn than it was outside. Mary's heart beat uncontrollably as she scanned the floor for the woodpile. When she found it, she put down the flashlight and quickly began picking up pieces.

Suddenly a loud creaking sound came from the wooden loft above her head. Something was up there. Mary wasn't going to stick around to find out what. Cradling a few pieces of wood to her chest, she ran out and up the dirt driveway back to the house.

Breathing hard, she put down the pile of wood near the stove.

"One more trip should do it," her dad said.

The words screamed inside Mary's mind.

ONE MORE TRIP!

"Can't this get us through the night?" she said, almost crying. "It's so creepy out there."

"Oh, Mary, there's nothing to worry about," her mom said. "The night's just playing tricks on you."

"Besides, it's good to face your fears," her dad said. "Get back out there, young lady, and face your fears."

A second later her parents were laughing at something on TV.

Mary went back out and then remembered she had forgotten the flashlight.

"That was stupid," she said, mad at herself and her parents.

She could see the small light in the barn in the distance. She forced her legs to move quickly down the dark path.

"Face your fears," Mary mouthed as she walked. "Face your fears."

As she reached the barn, the light went out. Mary took a deep, shaky breath and went inside. She felt around on the ground for the flashlight. After several seconds that seemed like minutes, she found it and gave it a shake.

The light flickered back on. But Mary's sigh of relief died in her throat as she looked down at the ground in front of her. Her mouth hung open and her eyes widened with terror.

The once neatly stacked woodpile was now scattered all over the floor. It took Mary a few moments to realize that the pieces were arranged in crude letters. Letters that spelled out...

Then the flashlight went out again and the door slammed shut.

"Have you come to face me, Mary?" a voice whispered in Mary's ear. "Have you come to face your fears?"

It was the voice of the thing she had felt and dreaded all along. It was the voice of the evil that haunted the place. A pure evil that now reached out its fingers for her from the darkest depths of the barn.

Mary stumbled forward and somehow managed to open the door. She ran toward the house screaming.

Behind her the red barn shook with wicked, unspeakable laughter.

Mary ran screaming.

She couldn't stop screaming.

Fool's Gold

It was too cold for September, Joseph thought, staring at the flames as they shot up into the black sky. He rubbed his hands together for warmth.

"All for nut'in'," Elroy muttered, spitting on the ground.

Joseph and Elroy had been searching for gold in the Klondike wilderness for the entire summer and the only things they had to show for it were callused hands and sore backs. With autumn closing in, they knew that they had better find their fortune soon or they would be heading back home to Seattle empty-handed.

"Take it easy," Joseph said. "We're not done yet."

"Not at all like they said," Elroy said. "Only ones making any money here are those mule packers and merchants selling us the equipment."

Joseph studied his grimy hands in the fire's glow.

"Gotta just keep working," Joseph said.

Suddenly, there was a loud rustling noise in the bushes behind them. Elroy stood quickly, stumbling a little as he reached for his rifle.

"Who's there?" Joseph yelled out into the darkness.

Both men breathed hard, staring at the brush. They had heard about men being attacked and killed by huge grizzly bears out here. The rustling got louder and then something walked toward them. But it wasn't a bear. It was a boy.

The men breathed a sigh of relief. Then Elroy got mad.

"Shouldn't sneak up on people like that, fool," he shouted. "Nearly got kilt."

He set his rifle down against a rock.

The boy was about 10, with dirty clothes. Joseph figured he must be a miner's son.

"What ya doing out here?" Joseph asked.

"My pa died a while back. I been living out here ever since."

"Out here all by yourself?" Elroy said.

He nodded.

"You hungry?" Joseph said, offering a biscuit.

But the boy refused the food. He sat down by the fire.

"Well, you ain't staying with us," Elroy said. "Can't be taking care of no stupid boy. We got work to do."

But Joseph didn't see it that way.

"You stay here with us tonight, help us mine in the morning and we'll bring you into town when we're through. Somebody there will help you out."

"Thank you, sir," the boy said.

"Your pa find any gold out here?" Elroy asked, eyes half moons.

"Yessir, lots. Big nuggets too," the boy said. "Pa was always lucky like that."

"Lucky 'til he wasn't, you mean." Elroy let out a long chuckle, and downed the rest of his drink. He stood up and stretched.

"This is what we're gonna do," Elroy finally said. "Tomorrow you gonna show us where your pa's claim is at. And if what you say is true, maybe we'll keep you on for a while. You know, take care of you some."

Joseph knew that Elroy was up to no good.

"Best get to bed now, son," Elroy said, handing him their extra blanket. "See you in the morning."

Joseph and Elroy secured the camp for the night in case of rain. The boy fell into a quick sleep next to the fire.

"Yeehaw," Elroy said in a low voice. Gold was dancing in his eyes. "Tomorrow the two of us gonna be rich!"

"Take it easy," Joseph said. "Let's just wait and see. And I think you mean the three of us."

"I mean what I said, two of us," Elroy said. "Don't be a fool. We ain't gonna keep this boy on. He's gonna show us where this gold mine is and soon after that it will be back to the two of us. You follow?"

Joseph stared at the sleeping boy. Never had he seen such a paler face. He crawled inside the tent, both excited and troubled about the coming day.

In the morning, the fog lingered, leaving the day cold and eerie. They gathered up their gear and followed the boy.

"Elroy, let's just take him back tonight," Joseph whispered. He had been thinking about it all night. "We'll take him into town and then his gold will be ours."

"No can do," Elroy said. A big sack of equipment hung over his shoulder. "He'll spill his guts like he done with us and a hundred miners will be here tomorrow."

They walked on. Joseph wasn't sure what to do. Maybe he should try to talk some sense into Elroy. Or at least warn the boy.

"Pa liked to dig up in those rocks over there," the boy yelled back to them, pointing to an outcrop.

Elroy smiled and rubbed the thick stubble on his chin.

"I'm gonna do this quick, partner. No sense in dragging it out."

Joseph was torn. He didn't want to see any harm come to the boy, but he really wanted that gold and didn't want to share it with anybody.

"In here," said the boy, disappearing into the mouth of a small opening. Elroy threw down his heavy load, held tight to his rifle, and motioned Joseph to stay back.

"I'll call out when it's all clear," he said, winking.

Joseph stood on the thin trail alone in the wet morning, waiting. He tried to feel excited about the gold, but he felt awful and guilty.

Suddenly loud, horrible noises came from the cave. Screams and howls and grunts and groans. Awful spine-tingling, blood-splattering sounds. Some crazed beast was ripping apart Elroy and the boy.

"ELROY!" Joseph screamed, running up to the dark entrance.

He stopped, frozen in fear. The noises were louder and even more horrible. He fired a shot into the air, but it didn't stop anything.

"Must have been a bear in there," Joseph whispered. His mouth was dry as bone dust and his heart thumped fast and hard in his chest. After a few seconds, he backed away. "Can't save nobody now."

Joseph started running down the trail. He was filled with fear, but it didn't stop his feet any. When he couldn't hear those awful sounds anymore, he stopped for a moment to catch his breath.

What if that man-killing bear follows me? Best to wait. I can get a good shot here.

He climbed up on a rock that overlooked the path and waited. It wasn't too long before he heard something coming.

"Dang, that was fast," he whispered, gripping his rifle.

Sweat poured from his face. Then he saw it.

It wasn't a bear. It was that pale, 10-year-old boy standing on the trail. Blood was dripping from his face. His shirt was ripped and stained. His eyes were huge and wild. He didn't look like any sort of boy anymore.

The thing stood there in silence, its long, red-colored teeth glistening through the fog as he sniffed the air.

And at the very exact moment that Joseph realized that the thing was looking for him, their eyes met. The rifle smashed to the ground as the boy raced toward Joseph. Soon, more of that terrible screaming could be heard for miles and miles.

And then it was quiet again.

Your Right...

An old woman walked by the cemetery one night and noticed a zombie rising up from its grave.

She hurried home and locked the door. She warmed up some old vegetable soup and slurped it down. After dinner, she went upstairs and got into bed. She put on her reading glasses and opened a book.

The wind pushed past the branches and the leaves and rattled the windows. And somewhere out in the night, a voice called out.

"Where's my small intestiiiiine?" it murmured in the distance.

The old woman put down her book.

"Who's got my tonsiiiiils?" it said, sounding a little closer.

The old woman pulled the covers tightly around her.

"Where's my appendiiiiix?" the voice groaned, just outside the front door.

The old woman shivered with fright.

"Where's my left kidneeeeey?" it said, now from inside the house.

The old woman held her breath.

"Have you seen my spleeeeen?" the voice moaned, coming up the stairs.

The old woman was about to have a heart attack when she suddenly remembered something.

"Hey, you're a zombie," she shouted as the zombie knocked down her bedroom door. "You don't need any of those things!"

"Your riiiiight—" the zombie said, shuffling toward the bed.

"I know I'm right," the old woman said as the zombie leaned over her.

"No, you didn't let me finish," the zombie said, taking a bite. "Your right... arm-*mmm!*"

Addy Lee

John Kilbane brought the autographed books with him to the school. The librarian had emailed the writer a long list of students who had bought his latest collection of ghost stories.

After the presentation, the librarian thanked John Kilbane and handed him a check.

"Thank you," Kilbane said.

"No, thank *you*," the librarian said. "I've never seen the students so excited about a book!"

Kilbane nodded and turned to leave.

"Oh, wait," she said. "Here's an extra one. I double-checked the list and no one by this name ordered a book. In fact, we don't have a student named Addy Lee."

She handed him the book and John Kilbane opened it to look at the name on the dedication page. There it was: *Addy Lee*. Maybe it got mixed up with another order, he thought. He put the book in his briefcase and walked out into the parking lot.

Back in the library, Ms. Deerfield told her ancient assistant about the author visit.

"The students just loved him," she said. "Strange about Addy Lee's book."

Old Mrs. Stern stopped what she was doing and whispered, "No…"

Pale as a corpse, she then collapsed to the floor.

"An ambulance is on its way," Ms. Deerfield told her a few minutes later when she had come to. "You gave me a real scare."

"I guess I scared myself too," Mrs. Stern said. "The last thing I remember was you saying—no, it couldn't be—saying something about Addy Lee."

"That's right. That's the name the author mistakenly signed in one of his books," Ms. Deerfield said. "I told him we didn't have anyone here by that name."

"That's where you're wrong," Mrs. Stern said, growing pale again. "We used to have a student here many years ago by that name. She was my best friend when I was a little girl. She died on the way home one day when the school bus slid on some ice and hit a tree."

At that exact moment, several miles away, John Kilbane's car was filled with a terrible, rotting smell and he heard the voice of a young girl coming from the back seat.

"I want my book," it said.

John Kilbane looked in the rearview mirror and couldn't believe what he saw. He turned around to have a better look. Sitting there was a small skeleton wearing a light blue, old-fashioned dress. Long hair still clung to the tiny skull.

"Who-who-who are you?" John Kilbane stammered. "What do you wa-wa-want?"

"My name is Addy Lee," the skeleton said and smiled. "And I told you, I want my book."

John Kilbane's heart stopped. A moment later, the car hit a tree. It was the same exact spot where Addy Lee had died 67 years earlier.

La Llorona

Stanley was swimming with Miguel, his best friend, down by the river. It was hot and the water felt right as the sun started to go down on this last day of September. Suddenly Miguel ran out of the water.

"Where you going, son?" Stanley asked.

"Gotta get home before *La Llorona* gets me," Miguel said.

"Is that the story about the crying woman who's always looking for her dead children?" Stanley said.

"It's no story, man," Miguel said, putting on his shoes. "She's real. My uncle said he saw her and the next day he died."

"All right, whatever," Stanley said, shaking his head. "See you at school tomorrow."

Miguel had once told him how the ghost of this tall, thin woman dressed in white would appear after dark. She would take kids who stayed out too late or who didn't listen to their parents. Sometimes she would appear to people before they died.

Stanley floated on his back staring up at the sky as the gentle current carried him. He wasn't thinking about *La Llorona*. He was thinking about his favorite thing: money. He loved holding it and counting it and he loved thinking of new ways of making it.

The next day, he came up with an idea. There were a lot of Hispanic kids like Miguel at school, and Halloween was coming up.

"One *hombre*'s scary story is another man's gold mine," he muttered to himself.

He wasn't sure what he was looking for but after visiting a few discount stores, he found it. It was a cheap plastic letter *Y*. He bought several dozen. When he got home, he tied a length of yarn to one of the letters. That was that. All he had to do now was give it a name and convince people they needed one.

"Yo Ro-Na Be Go-Na," he said. "That's it, Yo Ro-Na Be Go-Na!"

The next day before school, he paid some kids to start saying they had actually seen *La Llorona*.

"Say you saw her down by the river at night," he said. "She was dressed in white and crying and almost got you. Tell the story in class during your share time and at recess and lunch. Act scared, like it's real."

In the next few days, the stories started spreading through the school like a zombie plague. Pretty soon, everyone was talking about *La Llorona*. A lot of kids were actually scared. Stanley's plan was working to perfection.

The following Monday he set up a little stand with his necklaces.

"All you have to do is wear it and say *Yo Ro-Na Be Go-Na* three times and she can't get you," he said in his best salesman voice. "Only three dollars. And if it doesn't work, you get your money back."

He sold them before and after school and during recess and lunch. By the end of the week, he had made $339.

"This ain't cool, man," Miguel said to him a few days later. "My mom says you're playing with fire. You shouldn't mess with things you don't understand."

"All I understand is that I'm making a real killing," Stanley said, patting the big wad of cash in his pocket.

By Halloween it seemed that almost every kid in the school had bought the *Yo Ro-Na Be Go-Na* necklace and Stanley had made almost a thousand dollars.

When his mom took his younger brother and sister trick-or-treating that night, Stanley stayed home. He counted and recounted his money. Then he took a bath.

"And tomorrow's that—what's it called?—*La día de los muercos* or something," he said to his plastic duck. "Day of the Dead. I'm sure to sell some more."

Just then, Stanley thought he heard something outside the bathroom. It sounded like someone sobbing. And then it was quiet again.

An icy chill suddenly filled the room. Stanley shivered in the warm water. The lights went out.

"Mom," he called out. "Mom!"

But he remembered he was alone in the house. He heard the crying again. And then he saw her standing by the door.

Her white dress glowed in the dark. Her dark hair hung down over her sad, ghostly face. She floated closer to the tub.

"*Yo Ro-Na Be Go-Na, Yo Ro-Na Be Go-Na, Yo Ro-Na Be Go-Na,*" Stanley repeated as he held up his *Y* necklace.

"*Eso no sirve, mi hijoooooooooo,*" she moaned. "It is tooooo late for that and it is tooooo late for yoooooooooooooooooou..."

La Llorona was now right over Stanley.

"You're not re-re-re-real," Stanley stuttered, tears streaming from his bulging eyes.

A bony hand pushed his head under the water. He tried to fight, but it was no use.

"No llores, mi niño," she whispered sadly. "Don't cry now. Sleep, my child. Sleeeeep…"

Dead Man's Cave

"You got no shot with Chelsea," Rick said. "She's way out of your league, bro."

"We'll see," Adam said.

The two friends had been on the hot and dusty trail for three hours now. They were heading to Lake Podimouth up in the MacLamour Wilderness.

"Let's take a break," Rick said. "This pack is murder."

He propped up his heavy backpack against a tree and sat down on a large rock. Adam looked around as he drank some water. He spotted something nearby.

"Looks like a cave," he said. "Let's check it out."

"You go ahead," Rick said. "I'll rest here."

Adam dug out his flashlight and headed toward the opening.

"Be back in a few," he said.

Rick sat there eating a candy bar and looking at his map.

"Here it is," he mumbled. "*Dead Man's Cave*. How original."

A minute later he heard a loud crash coming from the cave followed by several echoes. Rick began to worry, but a few seconds later he saw Adam step out of the dark cavern.

"What was that noise, man?" he said.

"Huh?" Adam said. "Oh, I don't know."

Adam didn't say much after that. Rick thought that maybe he was mad because of the Chelsea thing, or because he didn't go with him inside the cave, or maybe he was just tired.

The hours and miles dragged on. But when they finally arrived at the lake in the late afternoon, it seemed a just reward for all their hard work. It was an epic spot, surrounded by snow-capped mountains, and they had it all to themselves. Even the mosquitoes left them alone. The only problem, as far as Rick could see, was that Adam was still quiet and strange.

After the first stars came out, they went inside the tent. Adam fell asleep the second he zipped up his sleeping bag. Rick followed a few minutes later. But something woke him during the night. It was Adam. He was weeping in his sleep.

"I want to live," he cried. "I want to live."

"Wake up, man," Rick said, shaking him. "Wake up."

Adam kept sobbing. Then he turned to face Rick.

Rick almost screamed out loud when he saw Adam's horrible expression. His red, bloodshot eyes seemed frozen with a kind of terrible confusion and fear. His face looked gray and lifeless.

"Don't leave me here," he moaned, grabbing Rick's arm.

"What are you talking about?" Rick said. "You just need to wa—"

Suddenly, Adam began to fade away right there in his sleeping bag!

"Don't leave me here," he kept sobbing as more and more of him disappeared. "I want to live."

The last to go were the eyes. Those terrible eyes, just

floating there. And then he was gone.

In the morning Rick woke up feeling exhausted.

"Man, I had a crazy nightmare last night," he said, turning toward Adam.

But Adam wasn't there, and all his things were gone. Rick packed up, not sure what to think. He headed back to the parking lot.

As the miles passed under his boots, Rick still couldn't make any sense of it. Could Adam really be so angry that he would just pick up and leave without saying a word? And over what? It just didn't add up.

When he reached the spot where they had stopped the day before, Rick saw a backpack by the side of the trail. It looked like Adam's.

Then he heard a voice coming from inside the cave.

"Don't leave me here," it whispered. "I want to live."

His heart racing, Rick ripped through his pack looking for his flashlight.

"C'mon," he said. "C'mon."

He finally found it and ran to the cave.

Adam was inside, about 20 feet from the entrance. He was down on the ground. His red, bloodshot eyes were open and staring out at the blackness. He had the same terrible expression as the night before.

It looked like he had been killed instantly by a falling stalactite.

Rick reached down to close his friend's eyes. Adam's face was ice cold. It felt like he had been dead for several hours—*maybe even as long as a day.*

I So Saw That Coming

Justin's friends decided to play a trick on him for his birthday. Jarrod distracted him after school while the three others raced over to his house and snuck into Justin's room through an open window.

"What do you want for your birthday? How old will you be next year? What's your favorite color?" Jarrod asked.

Justin became suspicious.

Why is he asking me all these dumb questions? he wondered. *Something must be up.*

"I've got to go," he said, starting for home.

When Justin got to his house, he went to his room to drop off his backpack and change. Jerry was hiding under the bed. Jason was in the closet behind some hanging shirts. Jermaine was behind a chair. They were all wearing clown masks.

The three friends had agreed to count to ten in their heads the moment Justin entered the room. Then they would pop out.

"Surprise!" Jerry shouted, grabbing Justin's leg when he neared the bed. Justin stumbled and fell.

"Surprise!" Jason screamed a second later, leaping from the closet.

"Surprise!" Jermaine bellowed as he jumped out from behind the chair.

They all started laughing. All of them except Justin.

Pale as a white crayon, Justin crawled over to the corner. He just huddled there, rocking back and forth, nodding his head.

"I *so* saw that coming," he mumbled. "I *so* saw that coming. I *so* saw that coming. I *so* saw that coming. I *so* saw that coming..."

Since that day 10 years ago, Justin has not said anything else.

He sits on the floor in the corner of his padded room at the asylum and repeats those words over and over and over again.

"I *so* saw that coming. I *so* saw that coming. I *so* saw that coming. I *so* saw that coming. I *so* saw that—AAAAAH!"

All the Pretty Vampires

Vampires had taken over the world.

All the best-selling books were about vampires. All the top-rated TV shows were about vampires. All the biggest money-making movies were about vampires. All the beaches were deserted. Tans were out. Pale was in. All the kids wanted to look and dress like vampires.

Vampires were cool and *oh so pretty*. Everyone either thought of himself as a vampire or in love with one. It got to the point where vampires hardly even needed to bite anyone. They just fed off all the love. The whole world was under one big vampire spell.

The whole world except for Dr. Gordon "Gordo" Chubbs, that is.

Gordo was old school all the way. He grew up back in the day when you killed vampires because they were undead and evil. Vampires were ugly. Vampires were bad. They had to be staked. End of story.

Gordo worked day and night in his lab to come up with an antidote to this curse of the pretty vampires. After years and years of failure, he finally came up with the solution.

It was all about the mirrors. As everyone knew, vampires could not see their own reflection. But what if they could? That would change everything, Gordo concluded.

He came up with a serum that allowed vampires to see themselves. But he still had a problem. How would he get the bloodsuckers to take it? Most of them were too smart to knowingly bring about their own doom.

And then one day, it came to Gordo. He would put the serum in the water supply. Of course, vampires didn't drink water. But humans did. And vampires still occasionally feasted on humans. The cure would be transmitted through humans.

Vampires began to see what everyone else could: they were pretty. *Oh so pretty.* Some vampires had not seen themselves in centuries. It was all too much, too fast.

Vampires began standing in front of the mirror for hours and hours, hypnotized by their own undying prettiness. And it wasn't long before their heads started growing, expanding, stretching until—Kapow! Kaboom! Kasplash!—they exploded.

Dr. Gordon "Gordo" Chubbs had done it! He had found a way to stop the curse of the pretty vampires.

Of course, the head exploding thing didn't exactly kill the vampires. They just stumbled around without heads. But they were totally helpless and harmless. And they were ugly. A headless vampire loses its charm fast. Most of them walked around like this until the sun came up. And then, of course, they burned up. The few smart ones—and they had to be smart to have no head and still remember to stay out of the sun—the few smart ones who returned to their coffins by day died of malnutrition.

Meanwhile, the humans suddenly woke up from their long sleep.

"I can't believe I used to love these ugly, headless freaks," people would say.

And then townspeople everywhere—doing what townspeople everywhere did best—got out their stakes and mallets and combed the countryside.

"Kill the freaks!" they shouted. "Kill 'em all!"

Suddenly finding themselves without heads, love, or sunscreen, the vampires began to disappear in record numbers.

Statues of Dr. Gordon "Gordo" Chubbs started going up all over the world. And in the ruins of a dark castle in Germany, seeing his chance, a long-forgotten, pieced-together monster started spending a lot of time in front of his mirror trying to figure out ways to become pretty.

"Fire, *bad*," he would say, combing his hair. "Pretty, *good. Ummm*, pretty, *gooooood.*"

Math Whiz

Sarah went outside to get the mail. She pulled out a blue envelope from the mailbox. It was written to her and had no return address. She hardly ever got any mail. Just a card from her grandmother once a year. But her birthday was in February, not July.

A warm wind blew through her hair. She opened the letter.

"Dear Sarah, See you in 5 days," was all that was written.

The next day after basketball practice, she found another blue envelope on her bed.

She opened it up.

"Dear Sarah, See you in 4 days."

A chill went down her spine. Goose bumps covered her arms. Who was sending these? It must be one of her friends having some fun, she thought.

The next day at the mall, her friends denied sending her the letters.

"I mean, really, I would just text you," Annabelle said.

"Not me," Quentin said. "I don't even know where to buy stamps."

As she walked home, she saw the postal carrier next to her mailbox.

"Good timing, girlie," the woman said. "This one's for you."

Her heart raced as if the game was on the line and she was shooting a three-pointer. She took the blue envelope and went inside the house. She opened it slowly.

"Dear Sarah, See you tomorrow."

"Tomorrow? What a jerk!" Sarah shouted. "Can't even count!"

Her friends laughed the next day as they passed the letters around.

"Probably somebody who failed math," someone said.

"Yeah, it's your future husband, Sarah," someone else said.

They kept on laughing, but Sarah felt queasy and worried that the enchilada she had just eaten for lunch would rise up and explode from her.

She walked home in the summer heat, sweat pooling on her upper lip. A few times she thought she heard footsteps behind her, but when she turned around no one was there.

When she got home, she found Scott Smith sitting on the front steps. She hadn't seen him since school had let out almost a month before.

"Hey, Sarah," he said, smiling.

"Hey, Scott," she said, wondering what he was doing on her porch.

She got her key out.

"Wait a minute," she said, putting things together. "Is it you? Are you the one sending those awful letters?"

She was mad now, could feel the rage burning in her blood.

"Yup," he said, grinning. "And here I am. Want to shoot some hoops?"

"For the love…" Sarah muttered as she pushed past him toward the front door.

"By the way, you scared me half to death," she said, turning around.

But Scott was gone.

"Guess I hurt his feelings," she said to no one. "Serves him right."

Relieved at least that the mystery was solved, she poured herself a large glass of lemonade and went to watch television.

That night Sarah was on the phone with Darcy.

"Hey, wasn't Scott Smith in your math class last year?" Sarah asked.

"Yeah, he was," Darcy said. "Why?"

"Was he bad at math?"

"Yeah, poor guy was no genius," Darcy said. "But I suppose it doesn't matter now."

Sarah explained that Scott was the one who had been leaving her notes and that he had visited her that afternoon.

"I don't think that's very funny," Darcy said. "You shouldn't say stuff like that."

"Why?" Sarah said. "What are you talking about?"

"You must have heard," Darcy said. "Scott Smith died in a skateboarding accident *last week*."

Sarah's blood went ice cold before she fainted and fell to the ground.

The Diary of Flem Smith

6 *September, 1620…* Our ship, the *Mayflower*, has set sail for America. It will be a long voyage. I do not understand why we had to leave Holland. I was born in England, but Holland is the only home I can remember. I miss Femke, my best friend. Father says the Dutch are not like us. I do not understand why that is a bad thing.

17 September… I have not vomited for two days.

22 September… A strange man from Holland is on the ship. His name is Jan Boemann. He only speaks a few words of English. He is very thin and tall. He dresses in black from head to toe except for the large white ruff around his neck. This collar is so ghastly and white, it hurts the eyes. Stranger still is that no one has seen Jan Boemann in more than a week.

30 September… People say now that Jan Boemann must have fallen overboard.

4 October… It is always night and loud down here. The wind and the waves and the coughing and the vomiting and the other body noises fill the foul air. The darkness hides the bugs in the biscuits. Nothing hides the smells. Such wretched smells.

9 October… A most heinous sailor has died. He would say awful things. Father says he was no better than the lice and fleas that crawl over our heads and bodies. Still, I am filled with sorrow at his passing.

11 October... The storms have been bad. Our tiny ship is tossed about on this great ocean. We are taking on water and there is talk we may have to turn back. I fear we may sink to the bottom of the sea.

14 October... The *Mayflower* has been repaired. The captain is confident we will reach America.

16 October... It was my turn again to go on deck and empty the bucket. It takes all of my concentration to keep the vile thing upright as the ship rocks from side to side.

19 October... One of the men fell into the sea during a storm, perhaps like Jan Boemann, but he managed to hold on to ropes and was pulled up to safety.

6 November... A servant boy died today. He is the second. Somehow, I do not think he will be the last.

9 November... Land! Land ahoy! We have reached America.

27 November... The men have been searching the coast for a place to build our new home. They have seen savages in this wild land. I wonder what new and strange animals we will encounter as well.

4 December... It is hard to see land so close and to have to stay aboard this miserable ship. Oh, to walk in those woods would be such a thing. I am not afraid of the cold or the savages. If only I knew how to swim. If only the waters were not freezing. I would do it. I would.

22 December... The men have finally found the spot. They will build the town by day and return to the ship at night. The icy sky screams with wind and snow.

29 December... John Poundstone returned today with a strange story. In the distant trees he saw a thin, tall man

dressed all in black. It was Boemann, he said. It could not be. But it was. As John approached, he saw that the large ruff around his neck was now dark red in color. His eyes were also red and his teeth and fingers had grown long and pointy. Father says it is the fever talking.

1 January, 1621... John Poundstone died today. His last words: "The Boemann is coming for me."

3 January... The snow falls silently on the dark water. December took with it six souls. The new year already two. They bury the bodies on the hill.

15 January... We are finally on dry land and off that terrible ship. We all live together in a common house. It is no bigger than the *Mayflower*, but we are on dry land. Finally, dry land. I thought I would be happier and, yet, I am troubled. I sense a darkness I cannot explain. A darkness blacker than night.

19 January... The story of Boemann will not die. It is said now he is here with us. Some of the older children have taken to singing a song: "If the scurvy or the cold do not take you, The Boemann will."

23 January... Little Jonas Gutkind's screams filled the night. "No, don't let The Boemann take me!" It was plain to see there was no one there. But Jonas saw him just the same. His little eyes still bulged with terror after he was cold and dead.

February 28... No one is singing anymore. Fully one quarter are dead. Many more will surely follow. It is cold here. So cold.

7 March... Terrible storms with no end. The world is white and The Boemann is real. I swear it. I saw his eyes last night in the dark. I was too weak from coughing to scream. I shake from fever and see him in my sleep still.

15 March... I saw The Boemann again last night. His long fingers stretched out for me. He smiled at me with his long, sharp teeth. And then he whispered in my ear, "Do not be afraid. Do not be afraid. Do not be a... AAAAAAH!!!"

Almost half of the 102 passengers on the Mayflower died during that first winter in America. They died of cold, hunger, and disease. It is not known how many were taken by The Boemann.

Not Joaquin

There was a creepy old hotel in a very scary part of San Francisco.

"We only have one room left," the hotel clerk said one night. "But it's said to be haunted by the head of Joaquin Murrieta."

"I'll take it," the man said.

As the man was falling asleep, he heard a terrible moaning coming up through the floor. And then a bloody head suddenly started floating in the middle of the room.

"No soy Joaquin," it wailed angrily. "I'm not Joaquuuuuuin."

The man ran out screaming.

The next night another guest was staying in the room. Just as the man was about to fall asleep, he heard the moaning coming through the floor. And then the bloody head appeared.

"No soy Joaquin," it cried as it floated in midair. "I'm not Joaquuuuuuin."

The man screamed and jumped out the window.

The following night a famous ghost hunter checked into the hotel.

"I want the haunted room," she told the clerk.

"It's all yours," he said.

The ghost hunter got in bed and started reading a book about the famous Joaquin Murrieta.

According to the book, Joaquin Murrieta was either a hero or an outlaw or both. To some people, he was a sort of Mexican Robin Hood. But to the governor of California at the time, Joaquin Murrieta was a murderous bandit. The governor offered a $5,000 reward for his capture—dead or alive.

In 1853 a man thought to be Murrieta was shot and killed. To prove that they had their man, the posse cut off the dead man's head and put it in a jar filled with alcohol. Some people said it was Murrieta, but others disagreed.

The head became the most famous head in California. It was taken from town to town and people would stand in line and pay to see it. Later it was displayed in a San Francisco museum until it was lost in the earthquake of 1906.

"And this hotel was built on the very site where the head was last seen," the ghost hunter said. "Fascinating."

Suddenly, the moaning began. And then the head rose up through the floor.

"No soy Joaquin," it said as it floated in midair. "I'm not Joaquuuuuuin."

The ghost hunter slowly closed her book.

"No soy Joaquin," the head wailed again. "I'm not Joaquuuuuuin."

"Honey, I don't blame you," the ghost hunter said, reaching for the phone. "Let me call you a taxi. I wouldn't be caught dead *walking* these streets at this time of night either."

For the ending to work, the reader needs to make sure that the name Joaquin is pronounced "wah-keen" throughout the story.

The Old Theater

The phone rang.

"I'm on my way," Dr. Childs said, her eyes looking away from her sons.

Courtland and Chip had been waiting all summer for *Man of Lead II*. From the trailer, it looked like it was going to be even more *sick* than the original. Today was the premiere and they were all ready to go.

"I'm so sorry, fellas, but Mrs. Matthews has gone into labor," Dr. Childs said. "I'll make it up to you."

The two boys didn't say anything.

A few minutes later they were riding their bikes in the hot afternoon sun and talking about how much it sucked to have a doctor for a mom.

"Stupid Mrs. Matthews and her stupid baby," Courtland said. "I hope it comes out super ugly with its butt where its face should be."

"Hey, you know it would be cool if these bikes were really motorcycles," Chip said. "That way we could go see the movie by ourselves."

"Yeah, but they're not," Courtland said. "So wake up and smell the *caca*."

The boys rounded a corner. And that's when they saw the sign.

"Now Playing... *Man of Lead II*."

"Would you look at that?" Courtland yelled, bringing his bike to a screeching stop. "I didn't even know this place was open again."

They were in front of the *Theater California*, the old downtown movie house, which had been closed for as long as Courtland and Chip could remember. But here it was, open and playing *Man of Lead II*.

"It's meant to be, son!" Courtland said.

They got off their bikes and walked up to the ticket booth. The next showing was in five minutes. Courtland bought two tickets.

When they reached the entrance, Chip suddenly stopped.

"You know what kids at school say about this place," he said.

"They're idiots, Chip," Courtland said. "And I don't care if this place *is* haunted. Today it's haunted in a good way."

A girl stood by the door dressed in clothes that made her look like she lived at a costume shop.

"Hey, how long has this place been open?" Courtland asked excitedly.

She didn't seem to hear him. She just took their tickets.

The theater was extra dark and empty.

"This place is kinda scary," Chip said, looking around.

"Change your diaper," Courtland said.

But even though he wouldn't let Chip know it, the theater gave him the creeps too. He started thinking about the stories surrounding the place. How it had been shut down because of unexplained disappearances.

They sat down in the middle of a row near the front. A minute later the curtain went up.

The movie was awesome, with even more *killer* action scenes than the first.

"That was soooo coooooool!" Courtland said as the credits started rolling.

But when he looked over, Chip wasn't there. In all the excitement, Courtland hadn't noticed that his brother had left.

Must have gone to the bathroom, he thought.

"What's taking so long?" Courtland said after several minutes. "Maybe the fool's waiting for me out front."

He stood up and shuffled sideways down the row of seats. A sharp bolt of pain suddenly shot up his spine.

"Guess that was a long movie," he mumbled, reaching for his back.

The pain only got worse as he slowly made his way up the aisle. When he turned down the hall, he saw the costume girl again. She had her back toward him.

"Excuse me, miss?" Courtland called out. "Have you seen my little brother?"

Again, she didn't seem to hear him. He walked up and tapped her on the shoulder. When she turned around, Courtland's jaw dropped. He almost fainted.

The girl's flesh was now a putrid shade of gray. Purple and green drool ran down her chin. She was an old woman—a *dead* old woman!

Courtland hobbled past her as fast as he could. Just as he was about to open the glass door that led outside, he heard someone call his name.

"Courtlaaaand," an old voice said. "What's happening, Courtlaaaand?"

Courtland turned around. An old man was coming toward him. He was ancient and bald with large freckle splotches covering his head. And he was wearing Chip's clothes.

"What did you do to Chip?" Courtland shrieked, the terror exploding in his voice.

The old man looked confused, and then scared. And as Courtland looked into his glassy eyes, he saw a familiar expression.

The old man *was* Chip.

Courtland screamed and then the old thing that was Chip began screaming too. Courtland turned toward the door.

If he could only get outside. If he could only get past the door. Then everything would be all right, he told himself. Everything would be fine.

And then Courtland caught a glimpse of his own reflection in the glass door. An old man was looking back at him.

Dr. Childs returned home that night to find her sons gone. The police searched all over town for them, but they didn't think to look in the old movie theater. After all, it had been closed for more than 30 years. It was closed still.

The two boys were never seen again.

Hit the Road, Jack

"Make sure to cut away from you," Ana's dad said. "So you don't hurt yourself."

"Okay," Ana said.

Ana held the fine-toothed saw tightly as she plunged it into the soft, orange flesh.

Carving pumpkins was one of Ana's favorite things to do. She could hardly wait for October. Every year the pumpkin she carved was more frightening than the year before.

She removed the lid.

"And now, *vee vill* operate on the patient's brain..." she said, laughing at her mad scientist joke.

A few hours later, Ana and her dad stood in front of the house in the dark, staring at her creation.

"Wow, Ana, for sure that's your best one yet," her dad said. "It looks horrifically frightening!"

It had been a long soccer practice for Jeff Keating. He was frustrated at having been shut down during the scrimmage by the defense and by his own teammates' lack of skill.

"Nice one, turd," he had shouted at his own goalkeeper as he watched yet another ball get by him and roll to the back of the net.

It was getting dark as Jeff climbed the street that led up to his house. A large, pale moon was rising over the neighborhood and dead leaves blew across the sidewalk.

Still upset, Jeff felt a terrible need to kick something. And to kick it hard. That's when he saw it there on the porch of a house. Looking extra stupid and just asking for it.

Jeff walked up quietly, grabbed the jack-o'-lantern, and headed back to the street.

"He shoots! He scores!" he shouted a second later, kicking the pumpkin with all his strength. He watched it break into a dozen pieces as it hit the asphalt.

Jeff felt much better the rest of the way home.

The next day was a good day. Jeff aced his math test at school, had lunch with Rebecca Westbrook, and scored three goals during soccer practice.

The sun disappeared from the sky as Jeff walked back home. Strolling along the quiet streets, he felt happy and full of energy.

Then something caught his eye.

He noticed a pumpkin on a porch. There was nothing strange in that—it was October after all. But there was something eerily familiar about this pumpkin. He had seen that face before. A candle burned in it, sending shadows ricocheting off the walls of the house. As he stood staring, Jeff felt certain it looked identical to the one he had splattered all over the street the night before.

"That's weird," Jeff said, walking quickly by the house. A gust of wind blew down the street, kicking up leaves and dust.

"Maybe some kids worked together, did two of them," he said, walking on.

Half way down the next block, Jeff stopped abruptly.

"It can't be," he said out loud, startling himself with the shakiness of his voice.

In front of a red house the same jack-o'-lantern sat glowing and smiling at him.

"This is ridiculous," Jeff said. "Someone must have seen me kick that pumpkin yesterday and wants revenge. This kid must be some loser to care this much about a stupid gourd."

As Jeff talked to himself, he turned up the street where he lived. He was almost home. He thought of all the things he would do. He would eat a big plateful of spaghetti sprinkled with at least half a pound of Parmesan cheese. He would watch his favorite reality show on TV. He would call Rebecca.

He was jogging now, his soccer bag slamming into his butt with every step. He dug into his jacket pocket for his key.

And then he stopped dead.

There on the doormat by the front door was the pumpkin. The same pumpkin. There was a darkness that poured from deep in its core out through its features. And then the eyes came to life with an evil glow. It looked right at Jeff and laughed.

The jack-o'-lantern began rolling slowly toward him. Then as Jeff screamed, the pumpkin burst into flames and picked up speed. Jeff dropped his bag and took off running down the street.

At first he put some distance between himself and the pumpkin, but the burning, orange ball began to get closer and closer. Jeff could hear its cackling, demented laughter get louder with each step.

Toward the end, the pumpkin was so close that Jeff could smell its burning flesh mixing with his own scorching skin.

Jeff begged for mercy, but the jack-o'-lantern just kept laughing.

Pagliaccio

Mario was walking home late one night. He was exhausted. He had worked his day shift followed by his friend's night shift at the mannequin factory. Sixteen straight hours.

"That's the last time I do that," he mumbled. "The last time."

The streets were deserted. It was a clear, cold, and windy night. Mario pulled the hood of his sweatshirt tight around his head. The wind was blowing trash down the alleys and cutting into his face.

He heard a strange, far-off sound. At first Mario thought it was the wind. It had to be. But as he got closer, he realized that it was singing. It was the saddest sound Mario had ever heard. Horrible laughter and heartbreaking sobs mixed in with the Italian words.

"Laugh, clown, at your broken love!
Laugh at the sadness that poisons your heart!"

Mario's route home took him closer and closer to the terrible sound. It had to be coming from a radio or stereo, he thought. But as he turned a corner, Mario saw that he was wrong. There was a man dressed as a clown, sitting on the curb, with his face in his hands. He was singing and laughing and crying all at once. It seemed impossible, but that's what was happening.

A mixture of fear and pity gripped Mario as he slowly walked up to the man.

"What's the matter?" Mario asked, bending over the clown. "Can I do anything to help?"

The clown kept crying into his hands. Mario grabbed the man's shoulder and the clown turned toward him. He dropped his hands from his face and stopped singing.

Mario then saw that the clown had no makeup and no eyes and no nose, just a horrible mouth with thin lips that stretched from ear to ear!

Mario gasped and struggled for air as he stumbled away down the sidewalk. He ran faster than he had ever run in his life. At first he could hear the clown singing again somewhere far behind him.

"Laugh, clown, at your broken love!
Laugh at the sadness that poisons your heart!"

Then all Mario could hear was the beating of his own heart.

After running several blocks, he finally began to slow down. Walking again, he started to catch his breath. He almost began to think that he had imagined the whole thing. But that face, now forever burned into his memory, told him it had been real. It was *too* horrible to imagine.

He started to walk faster. He wasn't far from home, but on this night each block felt like a mile.

And then he saw it. A taxi was parked up ahead. It had its lights on.

"Why not?" Mario said to himself. "I deserve a break."

He slid into the back of the cab and told the driver his address. Mario looked out the window at the buildings going by. He felt better and began to get sleepy. But after a while, he realized something was wrong.

"Hey, you're going the wrong way," Mario said to the driver. "My house is in the opposite direction."

The driver didn't answer. He turned off the meter and kept driving the wrong way.

"Hey!" Mario shouted. "Turn this car a—"

A song came on the radio. The music sounded hauntingly familiar. Then Mario heard the singer's words.

"Laugh, clown, at your broken love!
Laugh at the sadness that poisons your heart!"

Mario put his hands over his ears and began screaming. The last thing he saw was the driver turn toward him.

Somehow, Mario hadn't noticed that he was dressed as a clown. But he now saw—saw too late—that the man's face had no makeup and no eyes and no nose, just thin lips that stretched from ear to ear!

Paaa-Teee

"This guy's bought it," Bruce Babbington said, pulling a tarp over the body. "He's got no head."

"Yeah, this one too," Ron Cornelius said. "He's still got a head but it's facing the wrong way."

"It's strange how the van's in pretty good shape," Babbington said. "Like they weren't going that fast. No way there should be such terrible injuries."

Babbington and Cornelius had seen their share of horrific accidents. The two paramedics had been partners for 11 years.

They began attending to the three other victims.

"These two in here look dead, blood and brains all over the place," Cornelius said from the back of the van. "But somehow their vitals are good."

"This one's got a strong pulse too," Babbington said, leaning over the driver. "Breathing's good."

Cornelius suddenly dropped his first aid bag.

"B-b-b-Bruce," he stuttered, pointing at the tarp.

Babbington looked over.

The headless body was moving. It was sitting up. It was alive!

"That can't be," Babbington whispered, his eyes the size of Ping-Pong balls.

Just then Cornelius felt something grab his shoulder. He turned around—and turned as white as sugar on snow. It was the other corpse, the one with the head twisted around facing the back of its body. It was standing there, trying to speak.

"Uuugh," it moaned. *"Paaa-teee."*

The headless body was now moving toward Babbington.

"It's the end of the world!" Cornelius shouted. "Save yourself, Bruce."

"Paaa-teee," the corpse repeated, its arms flailing. *"Paaa-teee."*

"The living dead have taken over," Babbington screamed, running down the road. "Aaaaaah!"

Cornelius tried to follow, but the dead thing had a death grip on him.

"Paaa-teee," it said again. "Don't be afraid. You see, at the time of the accident we were headed to a *paaa-teee*, a costume *paaa-teee*... dressed as zombies."

El Viejo de la Bolsa

Manuel flew through the air on the park swing, higher and higher, until there was only sky. Suddenly he lost his grip and fell, landing hard on his head.

It hurt for a moment, but then Manuel felt all right. He got up off the ground and looked at the color of the sky. It was getting late. He knew he had to hurry if he wanted to get home before it got dark.

"*El Viejo de la Bolsa* will get you," his grandfather used to tell him when Manuel was younger. "He takes *shildren* who don't come home for the dinner."

Then the old man would dig his strong fingers into Manuel's ribs and laugh. Manuel didn't laugh then and he wasn't laughing now. He didn't believe a lot of the same things he did when he was little. But this story of the *Sack Man* still had power over him. It wasn't something he would admit to his friends and by the light of day it seemed like just another one of those things adults told kids to get them to behave.

Either way, the light of day was dying and his friends were probably all safe at home.

Manuel took a deep breath and walked quickly, not looking at the growing shadows of the graveyard. This dirt path circling the cemetery was the shortcut he took whenever he stayed at the park too long. His *abuelito* was buried here.

Maybe he'll look out for me, Manuel thought. He smiled, remembering the way the old man would laugh.

That's when he saw him, out of the corner of his eye. *El Viejo de la Bolsa* was there, right there among the tombstones! Tall and thin and dressed in black. Just the way his grandfather had always described him. And he was coming after Manuel!

"Waaaait," a voice called behind him.

But Manuel didn't wait. He took off running. His lungs burned, but he didn't slow down until he was far away from the graves of *el campo santo.*

As the streetlights came on and his breathing returned to normal, Manuel started to feel a little silly. It had probably just been someone visiting a dead relative. Nothing to get all streaked in the shorts over, he told himself. Well, at least he was going to be home in time for dinner.

Suddenly and with no warning, a tall, thin man dressed in black appeared five feet in front of him. Manuel was about to take off running again when the man spoke.

"It's good to see you again, Manuel," he said.

Manuel knew that voice, but he hadn't heard it in a long time.

"*¿Abuelito?* What are you doing here?"

The man reached out his hand. Manuel took it. He wasn't afraid anymore.

"You hit your head pretty hard, Manny," the old man said. "It's time for us to take a little walk back to where you just came from."

As night closed in all around, Manuel and his grandfather walked back to the graveyard.

Live(r) and Let Die

Buster Whitaker had a routine.

"Liver, please," he would tell the lunch lady every day at school.

And every day, the lunch lady got him liver.

Since the other kids hated liver, they didn't much care what Buster had for lunch. But that changed one day in November.

"It's not fair," they started saying. "Why does he get to choose what he wants for lunch?"

Some of them started asking for liver just to see what would happen.

"Ma'am, I would like some liver, please."

"Sorry, Missy," the lunch lady said. "It's Taco Salad Day!"

José gave it a shot the next day.

"I would like liver today, please, just like my good friend, Buster," he said, pointing.

"Sorry, that was the last slice."

A small group of fourth and fifth graders huddled together by the wall ball courts at recess. Buster was over on the grass, alone as always.

"Liver every day must be in his contract," someone said in disgust.

"What contract?" Lil' Ray-Ray asked.

"It's a saying, dummy," Bro Jay said. "You know, like Buster wouldn't even come to school unless they had liver waiting for him. Like he's some big shot."

"I'm sick of this special baby treatment," someone else said.

"Hey," Bro Jay said in his whiniest voice. "I want a hot fudge sundae for lunch or I'm gonna cry."

He yelled that last part across the playground and the wind picked up his words and blew them right into Buster. Buster stared at Bro Jay. It was a stare that sent icy chills up and down Bro Jay's spine.

"Punk," Bro Jay muttered.

Lil' Ray-Ray knew that Buster was in for it now.

The next day the group stood together during morning recess.

"Lunch gonna be special today," Bro Jay told them.

Lil' Ray-Ray felt a little sick. He knew Bro Jay had snuck into the cafeteria earlier that morning and stolen all that slimy, disgusting liver. He knew that Buster Whitaker would have to settle for four-cheese macaroni like the rest of them.

"Liver, please," Buster said at lunch.

The red-haired lunch lady stammered and stuttered.

"Uh, uh, well, there's a little problem."

Sweat dripped out of her hairnet and down her doughy face.

"We will have your liver soon. Mary Ella is out picking it up right now. We seem to have run out. You just wait over there, hon."

Buster sat alone at a table, waiting.

"Hey, Buster. Did they forget about you?" Bro Jay said, breaking into a huge gut-laugh that filled the cafeteria. "Wanna share my lunch? Or will macaroni give you a rash or something?"

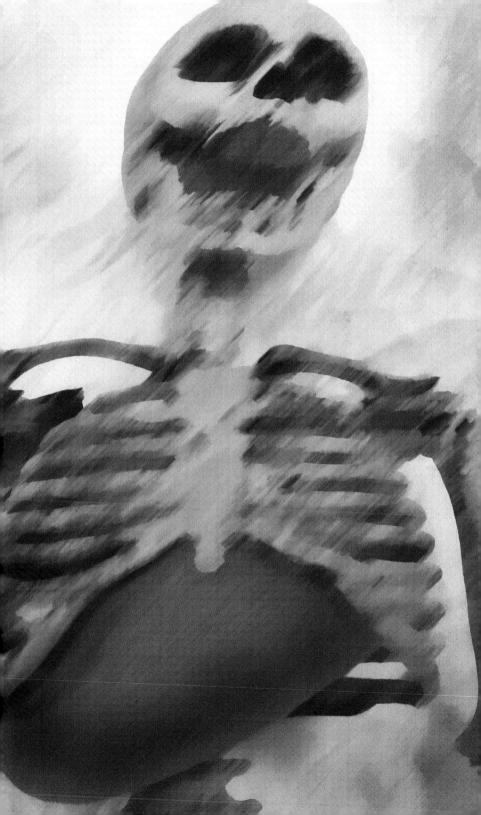

He went and sat down at the table across from Buster's. He dug his fork into his lunch and gave Buster a long look before he took a bite. He could see saliva running down Buster's chin.

"Sick, dude," Bro Jay said, watching gobs of drool drop from Buster's face. "Get yourself some macaroni—and a napkin."

Bro Jay took another bite. Suddenly, his stomach started aching.

"Ouch," he said, grabbing his gut. Buster glared at him and that seemed to make it worse.

The pain was throbbing. Not exactly his stomach, but next to it, right under his ribs. It burned.

"Maybe you got a point about not eating this macaroni, Buster. It's killing me."

"I want my liver," Buster said, staring at *Bro Jay's*.

Bro Jay didn't know what Buster was saying. All he could hear was his own groaning and moaning.

"Give me my liver!" Buster screamed.

He was still drooling, the slimy saliva dripping down his face.

"I want my liver," he repeated, his eyes as big as fat harvest moons.

Bro Jay looked at Buster and shivered. Then he lifted up his shirt and looked down at where the pain was coming from. It felt like something was pulling at him. He could see a growing bulge under his skin, next to his stomach. It was his *liver*! Buster was trying to steal it!

Bro Jay began screaming.

Buster just sat there drooling and pulling, drooling and pulling. Bro Jay kept screaming.

The House of Hearne

"All you have to do is bring back the dead bird before the sun comes up," Pete Molson said. "The map will show you where it's buried."

Murray and Freddy nodded.

"Any questions?" Pete Molson said.

"So we bring back the bird and we're members of the House of Hearne?" Murray asked eagerly.

"Yes, before the sun comes up," Pete Molson said. "We'll meet you down by the river at midnight."

Murray and Freddy went home and studied the map.

"Looks like it's about three miles to the island where the bird is buried and three miles back," Murray said. "It shouldn't be too bad."

"Do you think they killed the bird?" Freddy said.

"I don't know," Murray said. "And I don't care."

"And why do we want to join the House of Hearne again?" Freddy asked.

"'Cause there's two kinds of people in this stupid town," Murray said, starting to get mad. "House of Hearners and losers—and I don't want to be a loser, Freddy."

Freddy didn't want to be a loser, but he wasn't so sure he wanted to belong to this club either. If the House of Hearne Explorers Society was as awesome as Murray said, they should be digging for something cool like buried treasure instead of some poor dead bird, Freddy thought. But he knew how much it mattered to his older brother, so he kept his mouth shut.

As midnight approached, the boys packed a knapsack, put some pillows under the covers to make it look like they were sleeping in their beds, and slipped out the bedroom window.

It was a clear and chilly October night. Murray and Freddy walked quickly down to the river. The other boys were waiting for them.

"Here's a shovel," Pete Molson said. "Good luck and, oh, watch out for Davy."

Everyone knew the story of Davy La Boite. Davy La Boite was a boy who had drowned under the town's covered bridge almost 100 years earlier. His body was never found. Soon after the accident, the stories began to surface, each generation adding its own chapter. At some point the last name was changed to *LaBoo* and someone came up with a little nonsense rhyme: "Me and you and Davy LaBoo in the back of a smelly canoe."

According to some, Davy would rise up from his watery grave if someone stood on the bridge and spoke the words backwards. Others said that his ghost would get anyone who passed under the bridge at night without repeating the rhyme three times.

It was a moonless night and it took a few minutes for Freddy's eyes to adjust to the black water out in front of him. The paddle still felt cold in his hands as they approached the covered bridge. It loomed larger and more ominous with each stroke.

"Me and you and Davy LaBoo in the back of a smelly canoe. Me and you and Davy LaBoo in the back of a smelly canoe," Freddy whispered under the bridge's dark shadow.

"Me and you and Davy LaBoo in the back of a smelly canoe."

"Don't be such a child," Murray said from the stern.

"Ain't no Davy LaBoo."

Freddy paddled hard and with the help of the current they were soon through to the other side.

Suddenly a loud splash came from somewhere behind them.

"What was that?" Freddy asked nervously.

"Probably just a fish," Murray said. "No, I mean, *I'm the ghost of Davy LaBooooooo coming to get yoooooooou.*"

"Cut it out, Murray," Freddy said.

They made good progress down the river and reached the lake. Freddy sighed with relief when he saw the small island come into view.

"There it is," Murray said, pointing his flashlight down at the map. "The bird's supposed to be buried somewhere in the center of this island."

They pulled up on a gravelly beach.

"Get the shovel," Murray said. "Looks like a black rock marks the spot."

His flashlight cast creepy shadows as the trees closed in all around. Deeper and deeper into the woods they walked in search of the grave of the dead bird.

"There," Freddy finally said, pointing to a rock.

"I'll dig first," Murray said.

The dirt was soft. Soon the shovel hit something.

"Point the light down here," Murray said, getting down on his knees.

He dug at the dirt with his hands and pulled out an old, wooden box. He removed the lid.

"That's sick," Freddy said, looking down at the dead bird. It was a big black crow. Its eyes were open and bulging and seemed to be looking right at them. Goose bumps covered Freddy's arms.

Murray closed the lid and stood up.

"Let's get going," he said.

They walked quickly through the forest to the canoe. Murray carefully placed the box down under his seat. They paddled silently back across the lake. Soon they were back on the river. The bridge was up ahead.

All they had to do was get past this bridge and they were home free, Freddy thought. But he had a bad feeling. Dread, like hands closing in around his neck, began to choke him.

"Isn't there another way we can get back?" he said in a shaky voice.

"You know there's not," Murray said. "Suck it up, girlfriend."

"Me and you and Davy LaBoo in the back of a smelly canoe. Me and you and Davy LaBoo in the back of a smelly canoe," Freddy said again under the bridge. "Me and you and Davy LaBoo in the back of a smelly canoe."

"I told you there ain't no—" Murray said.

Freddy heard a loud splash behind the boat. A second later, the canoe rocked violently.

"Stop messing around, Murray," Freddy shouted. "You're gonna flip us."

Murray didn't answer.

"Murray? Murray!"

Suddenly a gruesome odor filled Freddy's nostrils. He turned around slowly. What he saw would stay with him for the rest of his life. There in the back of the canoe, a green-black mass of hair, bone, and rotting flesh stood over Murray. An eerie glow escaping from its empty eye sockets, the thing just stood there dripping with evil.

"Me and you and Davy LaBoo in the back of a smelly canoe. Me and you and Davy LaBoo in the back of a smelly canoe," Freddy repeated, shutting his eyes tight. "Me and you and Davy LaBoo in the back of a smelly canoe."

When he looked back again, the ghost of Davy LaBoo had wrapped its limbs around Murray. A moment later they both went over the side and disappeared. Bubbles rose to the surface. At first, Freddy thought he could hear screaming and hideous laughter coming from under the black water. And then everything was quiet again, like nothing had ever happened.

Freddy made it home that night and lived to be a very old man, telling the story to anyone who would listen. Murray was never seen a—GAAAAAAAAAAAIN!

The Ghost of Bruddah Stu

"The Ghost of Bruddah Stu haunts that beach to this day," Molly said. "The story goes that a giant wave hit him so hard, it ripped his head clean off his body. And they never found the head."

"Yeah, and his great ghost body wanders around at midnight of the full moon looking for his surfboard—and his missing head," Jessica added.

"Those are just stories," Linda said, taking a hit off her soda. "Just stories."

"My uncle said he saw the ghost one night when he was a kid," Anna added.

"Your uncle's been eating too much seaweed," Linda said. "Ghosts are like wrestling—they're just not real."

"Hey, there's a full moon tomorrow night," Molly said. "I'll give you $100 if you spend the midnight hour on that beach alone and show us how brave you are."

"$100?" Linda said, trying not to sound too excited. "You've got yourself a deal."

The next night Linda's friends took turns digging a deep pit in the sand with a shovel. It was hard work. They had decided to bury Linda up to her neck to make sure she really stayed at the beach. They would come back at one o'clock to dig her out.

"This hole is back far enough so you don't have to worry about the tide," Molly said after they had covered their friend and stomped down on the sand. "Bruddah Stu is the one you have to look out for."

"Yeah, yeah, yeah," Linda sighed.

"It's 11:53," Anna said looking at her watch. "We'll come back for you in just over an hour."

Linda watched her friends walk down the beach toward Jessica's house. The beach was deserted. A breeze blew through the sand as the moon climbed higher in the black sky. The waves pounded the shore. There were a few tiny lights out on the water from distant ships.

Linda's feet began to get cold. The sand down there was wet. She had a terrible itch on her nose she couldn't reach because her arms were pinned to her body. It was pretty uncomfortable, but she wasn't afraid. She passed the time thinking how she would spend her $100.

Nothing happened for a long time.

Then suddenly Linda heard splashing somewhere out in the water. A few moments later, she saw a large shape coming out of the ocean.

"It burns," the shadow moaned. "It buuurns..."

At first Linda thought it was just one of the other girls trying to scare her. But as the thing came closer, she could tell it was too big to be one of her friends. Whatever it was, it was heading right toward Linda. Her heart pounded hard against the sand. Her belief that there was no such thing as ghosts was disappearing faster than a sandcastle at high tide.

"It burns," it groaned again. "It buuurns..."

As the large figure closed in, Linda could now clearly see in the moonlight that it had a head. Bruddah Stu had found his head!

Of course it burns, Linda thought with what was left of her mind. *All that salt water seeping into that terrible wound has to burn something awful.*

The ghost was no more than 10 feet away and getting closer with each step. Too terrified to scream, Linda could only stare. Its skin appeared red in the moonlight.

"It burns," Bruddah Stu moaned again, now hovering over Linda. "It buuurns…"

Linda's heart almost stopped. She fainted right there in the sand.

A few minutes later, Linda's friends dug her out.

The *ghost* of Bruddah Stu turned out to be nothing more than a large tourist who had jumped in the water to cool off a bad sunburn.

The Girl Who Wouldn't Marry Nuno Neves

"**W**hen Portuguese explorers first saw coconuts it reminded them of the *Coco*, which was their word for a sort of boogeyman-ish ghost or witch," the history professor said. "So you see, because of its brownish, hairy appearance, the coconut was actually named after the boogeyman."

Julia yawned loudly.

"This guy's killing me," she said under her breath.

After class, a student named Nuno came up to her. He always sat in the back, filling up notebooks with hearts and Julia's name.

"This class I like and me like you," he said and smiled. "One day me marry you."

"Get away from me, you creep," Julia said. "Do they just let anyone into this university? I would rather marry—what's his name?—the *Coco*."

Nuno became quiet and looked at the ground. Julia walked away.

A few weeks later the professor made an announcement at the end of class.

"I'm sorry to inform you that one of our students, Nuno Neves, has died. I don't have any other details," he said.

I wonder what happened to that creep, Julia thought and then shook her head. *Must have died from a broken heart.* She had to force herself not to laugh.

The next day a sickly sweet odor filled the old classroom. Julia knew right away what it was because she hated that smell. The room reeked of coconuts.

"Makes me hungry for some curry," the professor said. "And a piña colada."

As the days went by, the smell got stronger and stronger. It started to follow Julia everywhere she went and people even began to think that it was coming from her, that it was some new shampoo or perfume she was wearing. It was on her clothes, her hair, and her skin. And no matter how much she showered or did laundry, it only got stronger.

Julia sat alone in the corner of the cafeteria one afternoon. Suddenly she spit out her milk.

"This tastes like coconut!" she said, looking at the carton and seeing that it was just regular, plain milk.

Soon everything Julia ate tasted like coconuts. She stopped eating and going to her classes. She just stayed in her room day and night.

Weeks later, Julia found herself on a hospital bed. A dark fog covered the room. She thought she heard that song they played at weddings and felt herself being lifted off the bed. She looked down and saw that she was wearing a white dress.

Julia floated down a long hall lined by skeletons. When she stopped, Death stood in front of her with his hood and scythe. In the other hand he held a burning book.

"We are gathered here…" he began.

Julia was too weak to fight, too weak to run, too weak to scream.

"You look lovely, my dear," a ghastly voice whispered in her ear. "The ring, Nuno."

Julia turned behind her and saw Nuno Neves hold out a ring in his gray, dead hand. Horrible, hairy fingers reached out for it. And then for Julia.

She saw the ring slip onto her finger.

"You may now kiss the bride," Death said.

The tuxedoed figure to her side turned and pulled Julia in tight.

Before closing her eyes for the last time, Julia saw the thing with the hairy and hideous brown coconut head lick its lips and...

AAAAAH!

Sketch

A monument to madness, the old State Mental Hospital sat on a hill overlooking the small town of Josephson, Oregon. Over the years, a lot of questionable experiments had been performed there. The hospital had been closed for more than 10 years now but, according to some, the screams could still be heard on quiet nights.

It didn't take long after the doors closed for the abandoned asylum to become a popular late-night destination for teenagers looking for a break from the boredom of small-town life. And it didn't take long for stories surrounding the place to sprout like the weeds that covered the dead lawn.

Shadows without explanations. The ghost of a young nurse who had gone down to the basement for some bandages and was never seen again. Bodies buried in unmarked graves in the woods behind the main building rising up at midnight. And, of course, the screaming.

But on this night, Ray and the other three boys were interested in something else.

They climbed the fence and crawled in through one of the many broken windows. Sam led the way since he had the only flashlight. They were headed to Room 202. Room 202 was supposed to be the room of one of the hospital's most infamous patients, Pierre "Sketch" Benoit. He got his nickname from the drawings of victims he left behind at crime scenes. The bodies were never found, just the sketches.

When he was finally caught, Benoit confessed to 27 murders. No one had any reason to doubt him—or that he was completely insane.

The boys sat in a circle. A candle flickered in the middle, throwing their shadows on the walls.

"Pierre, Pierre, appear from thin air," they began. "Benoit, Benoit, where are ya?"

"It's not going to work unless we hold hands," Bob said.

"Perfect," Ray sighed, sticking out his arms. "That's exactly how I wanted to spend my Friday night, holding hands with you losers."

"Pierre, Pierre, appear from thin air," they chanted. "Benoit, Benoit, where are ya?"

"Wait, I think I feel something," Sam said, leaning to his right. A loud noise bounced off the tile floor beneath him and a rotting smell filled the air.

"Sick, man!" Carl said. "Keep it to yourself."

After a good laugh, the boys went back to their chanting.

"Pierre, Pierre, appear from thin air. Benoit, Benoit, where are ya?"

After several minutes it became clear that nothing was going to happen.

"Pierre has left the building," Bob said, sounding disappointed. "I guess we weren't worthy."

Carl blew out the candle and Sam switched on the flashlight. They all stood up and shuffled toward the door, Ray bringing up the rear. Suddenly Sam turned around and pushed Ray back into the middle of the room. Then he slammed the door shut. The sound echoed up and back down the hall. It was as dark as the inside of a coffin in that cell.

From out in the hall, the boys laughed.

"Okay, good one, Sam," Ray said. "Real funny. Now let me out."

Ray pushed on the door and Sam pulled on the handle from his side, but nothing happened. It was stuck.

All four of them tried it.

"One, two, three…"

The door wouldn't budge.

"We'll look around for something to help pry it open," Sam said. "Sit tight."

"Where would I go?" Ray said. He heard the boys go down the hall and then it got quiet.

He could smell the smoke from the candle. *Too bad Bob's got the matches*, he thought.

After a few minutes, his eyes started to adjust to the dark. He could make out the bed and the crumbling ceiling and the door. He walked around and looked at some of the sketches that still covered most of the walls. It was all pretty creepy, but it would take a lot more to scare him. *I ain't some mama's boy*, he thought. Still, Ray wished his friends would hurry.

Then with a squeak, the door slowly swung open.

Ray was about to say something like "it's about time," when he noticed that no one was there. The door had opened by itself. He thought he heard someone whisper his name. Then he felt a chill pass through him.

A few minutes later, the other boys found Ray standing in the hall outside the room.

"Ray?" Carl said. "Is that you?"

"No, it's Pierre," Ray said staring past the light from the flashlight.

"I'm glad you still have a sense of humor about it," Sam said. "How'd you get out of there, man?"

Ray didn't answer.

Sam talked quickly and nervously during the drive back to town. He felt bad about playing that trick. Ray didn't say a word. He just sat there. To Sam it looked like he was far away, deep in thought.

"See you later, Ray-*der*," Sam said when they pulled up in front of Ray's house.

Ray didn't answer. Sam put his hand on his friend's shoulder. Ray turned to face him.

It's almost like he doesn't know who I am, Sam thought.

Ray then got out of the car and walked slowly toward his house.

"Must still be mad," Bob said as he took Ray's place up front.

"Yeah," Carl said from the back seat. "Hard not to be."

Sam wasn't so sure that was it.

Ray unlocked the door and went inside.

"Hey, Ray," his mother said from the living room. "Did you and your pals have a good time?"

He went up the stairs.

"Ray?"

Ray walked into his room without bothering to turn on the light. He sat at his desk and took out a notebook and a pencil. He stared out at the darkness. And then he started sketching Sam's dead face.

It's a Wrap

Billy Bob and Bobbie Jo were parked up where Old Mill Road dead ends at the southern tip of Lake Boudreaux. It was a quiet, moonlit night in late April—still too early for swimming but just right for pondering. The two sweethearts were talking about their plans after high school.

"I'm glad you're going to college," Billy Bob said.

"Wish you'd come too," Bobbie Jo said.

"I just don't kno—" Billy Bob said and stopped.

There was a loud whining sound and then a metal-meets-bone crunching followed by horrible screaming.

"What was that?" Bobbie Jo asked bug-eyed, sliding closer to Billy Bob.

"It sounded like it came from the old mill," he said. "But that place's been closed for years."

Everything was quiet again.

Then a few moments later a heavy thump rocked the bed of Billy Bob's pickup truck. When he and Bobbie Jo looked back, they couldn't believe their eyes. It looked like a body! It was just sitting there, wrapped in bloody bandages from head to toe.

"Help meeee," it moaned.

And then it started to move toward them.

"Get us out of here!" Bobbie Jo yelled.

Frozen by fear, Billy Bob could only stare.

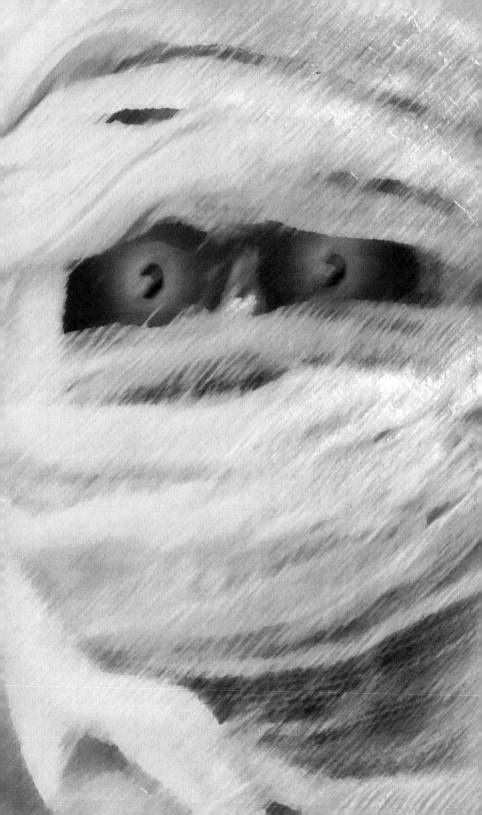

"Come on!" Bobbie Jo said, punching Billy Bob hard on the arm.

Billy Bob started the truck and took off.

The thing in the bandages moved closer and closer until it was just outside the window. Bobbie Jo could now see its face, covered except for the eyes. Those terrible eyes pleaded with her.

"Help meeee," it moaned again, pounding on the glass.

As the truck flew faster and faster down the winding road back to town, it hit a bump. Bobbie Jo bounced up and hit her head. When she looked behind her again, the thing wasn't there.

"I think it's gone," she said, breathless.

"What do you mean, gone?" Billie Bob said.

"It's not there," Bobbie Jo said.

"I don't care," Billie Bob said. "I'm not slowing down till we get to town."

A few minutes later, the pickup truck stopped at *Elmore's Gas 'n Git*. Billie Bob and Bobby Jo got out and walked slowly toward the back. There was nothing there. Billie Bob kept staring at the back of the truck.

"Did we just imagine that?" Bobbie Jo said.

Billie Bob shook his head.

"That would work except for two things," he said as he picked something out of the truck bed. "For starters, my 'magination's not that good."

"What's the other reason?" Bobbie Jo asked.

Billie Bob held up what he had just found in the back of the truck.

It was a bloody bandage.

Bonus stories from

They're Coming For You 3
Scary Stories that Scream to be Read... Thrice

(coming soon in paperback)

Field Trip

We stood around the giant tombstone. Nobody was bored and nobody was talking.

Julio knocked me in the side with his elbow.

"This is some strange field trip," he said.

The tombstone was standing upright on a table and a man was holding a hose that blasted sand into the granite slab, engraving it.

Julio was right. Mrs. Jones had sure topped herself this time: tombstone artist. Now that's a career.

"It's important to know the different career choices available to you," she had said at the beginning of the semester to our freshman class.

Soon the crazy field trips began. We went to a car dealership and the courthouse. Then to a bank, a bridal store, and an Italian restaurant. Now, at the beginning of spring, we stood in a large warehouse watching how tombstones were made.

The guy with the hose turned it off so our guide could speak.

"This one here is for Mrs. Edwards," he said.

The man was wearing a dirty blue apron, had a huge gut and long, gray sideburns that looked freakish.

"The sand is being blasted out at such a powerful force that it's able to cut through the thick granite. Granite is one of the strongest materials in our world, you know. This is the only way we can cut through it to engrave our product here."

In a few minutes the man had finished.

Edna Edwards
1919-2010
Beloved Wife, Mother, and Grandmother
In Our Hearts Forever
RIP

"Any questions?" Blue Apron asked.

Julio raised his hand.

"How much do these cost?" he said.

"It's all included in the mortuary package," Blue Apron said, annoyed. "Who else?"

"Do you know how Edna Edwards died?" James asked.

"Well, yes, we do, but we're not supposed to tell," Blue Apron said, looking around for our teacher.

Mrs. Jones was standing away from us, reading something on her phone. The man smiled and then whispered.

"Brain cancer. It just ate her brain away. Kind of like little bugs in there," he said, tapping his own skull.

"Okay, well, thank you," said Mrs. Jones. "Students, we need to move along. Tombstones aren't the only thing Michael's Engraving makes. Come on, out the door to the next building. Single file please."

I was last in line, waiting to move but it was taking forever.

Suddenly something touched my shoulder.

"What?" I said out loud, turning and expecting one of my friends. No one was there.

But there was something breathing in my face. The smell was horrible, like rotting flesh.

"Dude, do you smell that?"

But Julio was way ahead of me and kept on walking, following the line out the door.

"Who's there?" I asked.

I still heard the heavy breathing and then some words.

"Don't get on the bus."

It was an old woman's voice. I couldn't see her but she was right in front of me. Right there, breathing her foul breath into my face.

"Don't get on the bus, or you'll be in here with us!"

"What?" I said. "What are you talking about?"

Suddenly that putrid smell disappeared.

I ran, catching up to the rest of the line.

"That's a good one, " Julio said after I told him what had happened.

We were sitting on a patch of grass outside eating our lunches. The sun felt good and I was glad to be out of that horrible warehouse. Had I imagined it all?

Afterwards, we visited the trophy room and then it was time to leave. I looked back at the tombstone warehouse and that's when I saw her, standing in a window on the second floor and looking right at me. She was wearing a flowing blue dress, her head full of blackness, blackness where her eyes and mouth should have been. A bony finger waved back and forth.

"Don't get on the bus, or you'll be in here with us!" she screamed inside my head, over and over again.

I took off running. I heard Mrs. Jones yelling behind me, but it just made me run faster. I couldn't help it. I ran and ran and ran as I thought about that rotting head full of black holes.

It was starting to get dark by the time I made it up to my front porch.

My mom met me at the door. I knew I'd be in trouble. But there was something more.

"Dave?" she said.

She had been crying. Her face was red and swollen. Her eyes were tiny slits, pushed far back into her face.

"Sweetheart? Is that you?"

She came up nervously and started poking me.

"Of course it's me," I said.

I was exhausted. I figured I had probably run at least 10 miles. I was hungry too.

Suddenly, she gave me a crazy hard hug, squeezing me tightly as she cried.

"We were sure you were in the river," she said. "But you've been saved! You've been saved!"

The bus had never made it back from the tombstone factory. As it crossed the river, it skidded off the bridge and plunged into the water.

There were no survivors.

The Geek Shall Inherit the Earth

"Hey, Tomato Head, good weekend?" Cameron yelled as Jen passed by on Monday morning.

His friends, who were gathered around waiting for the bell to ring, all laughed.

For Jen Andrews, life had become as gloomy as the cold, wet winter that surrounded her each morning on the way to school. Nothing was going right. Her best friend had moved away. She kept getting bad grades on her math tests. And she started wearing large red-rimmed glasses that felt strange on her face.

Then, of course, there was Cameron: a mean, skinny fifth grader who took great delight in tormenting quiet and scared fourth graders every day before and after school. Lately, Jen had become one of his favorite targets.

"Hey, Bubble Butt, I'm talking to you!" he yelled.

Nothing ever stopped Cameron either. It seemed like the more teachers made him stay in for recess for "rude behavior," the more he lashed out, seeking revenge on whoever had spilled their guts.

One gray morning, Jen felt worse and worse as she walked to school. She kept thinking of all the bad stuff that was going on and couldn't think of any solutions. As she crossed the street, she felt a darkness start to grow inside her stomach. By the time she got to school, the strange feeling had spread throughout her entire body.

It was so powerful that as she rounded the corner and saw Cameron, all freckles and smirks, she didn't look to the ground like she usually did. Instead, she stared right into Cameron's mean eyes.

"Hey, Tomato Head. What's for lunch?"

Jen kept staring until Cameron looked away.

Strange, Jen thought. *He usually bugs me until I get to class.*

All day long Jen noticed that things seemed different. She didn't know what it was, but she liked how strong and brave she felt. She played soccer at recess and scored a goal. And in math, she finally learned how to divide. It was a great day!

But there was Cameron waiting for her on the sidewalk after school.

"Hey, Big Butt, wait up," he screeched, jogging over to her.

He was by himself.

"They'll have to fit your butt with glasses too so it can see where it's going," he said.

But surprisingly, Cameron's words had no effect on Jen like they usually did. They just rolled out of his mouth and fell to the ground. Inside, Jen just felt different. She stared at him, stared for a long time, saying nothing. She was so focused that she barely noticed that he had started crying.

"What did you do to me?" he screamed. "What did you do?"

As Cameron ran away down the street, Jen noticed that his own butt now seemed ginormously huge—far too big for his ripped pants.

She wasn't sure what was happening.

But she had a powerful feeling it was going to be a good year after all.

La Arrugada

Oh, good you are awake, my friend. We were about to start without you. How are you feeling? What are you in here for? What is your name?

You are right, Miguel. My apologies. So many questions. Where are my manners? Dear me, I fear that was another question.

Allow me to introduce myself. My name is Diego Cervantes. And that over there is Miguel Lavolpe. Miguel, as you can see, broke his leg. The doctor says he will be going home tomorrow. I am here because of, well, it is rather embarrassing.

Diarrhea.

I ate something that didn't agree with me three days ago and I haven't been able to stop going. I apologize in advance if I should wake you in the night with my rude noises.

In any case, Miguel and I like to tell stories to pass the time. Perhaps you would like to tell one of your own. Or simply listen if you choose.

I will go first.

This is the story of *La Arrugada*, The Wrinkled One.

No, Miguel, it is not about an old woman. Please, no more interruptions.

A very long time ago there was a young nurse who worked at this very hospital. Her name was Beatriz. She was a very good nurse, gentle and caring with her patients. She was the best nurse in the entire hospital. Beatriz did not perform miracles but her patients were the happiest patients in the hospital and many of them did get better, more so than the other nurses' patients.

The other nurses began to get jealous of this. And so they worked out an elaborate scheme to get even. They enlisted the assistance of a doctor at the hospital. He was very handsome.

The nurses started writing love letters to Beatriz from the doctor. With each letter, she became more and more intrigued and at some point fell in love with him. She began writing back. Finally, the doctor asked Beatriz to meet him on the roof one night.

There was a beautiful full moon and it was warm.

¿Qué? Yes, Miguel, just like tonight. Now, please, let that be the last interruption.

"Oh, doctor," Beatriz said sweetly. "I love you too."

Suddenly all the nurses came out of the shadows and started laughing. The doctor laughed too.

"Did you enjoy our little joke?" they asked.

"Well, back to work everyone," the head nurse said.

After they all left, Beatriz walked over to the edge of the building. She stared at the street below. It was a long way down. She thought about jumping. She thought about it for a long time. Eventually, however, she stepped back from the abyss and returned to work.

But as the days went by, she became sadder and sadder. She lost interest in everything. Even in her patients. She began to show up to work late with a dirty, smelly, and very wrinkled uniform.

Beatriz was eventually fired. She never recovered from the cruel joke and died soon thereafter.

About a year later, rumors started spreading throughout the hospital that a ghost was roaming the halls late at night.

Some said it was Beatriz looking to take revenge on the other nurses. Others said she was looking for the doctor. Some said she looked and walked like a normal person, while others claimed she floated and glowed with a ghostly malice.

All the stories agreed, however, on two points. Beatriz was no longer gentle and caring. She had become evil, consumed with a burning hatred. And she still wore the terribly wrinkled uniform.

Sometimes an unfortunate patient would make the mistake of interrupting the ghost, this *fantasma*, from her mission. When someone would call out in the night for help, the ghost would sometimes appear. And she would be most displeased.

Patients suddenly started dying in the hospital. And not just the ones in critical or grave condition. The ones in good condition too. Patients who had no business dying.

What's that? You are in pain? Oh, that is too bad. *Que lastima.* There is that switch by the side of the bed. Yes, that one.

The nurse will soon come with your medication.

Allow me to return to our story. It will perhaps help take your mind off the pain.

Unfortunately, there is not much more to tell. It is just a story after all, but some of the more superstitious insist that the ghost of Beatriz is real and that she returns with the coming of the full moon.

Wait. What was that? Out in the hall. Did you hear it? Did you hear the words?

"Doctor, is it you? *Te quiero, mi amor.* I still love yoooooou…"

It must be her.

[Whisper] *Por el amor de Dios*, do not make a sound. God protect us. She is coming. Our only hope is to pretend we are asleep.

The door is opening.

It is she, *La Arrugada*. She has answered your call. Do you smell the filthy uniform? Oh, no. Do not look upon her face. It is twisted with hate. Oh, and the wrinkles. The horrible wrinkles.

Save yourselves. Save yoursel—

AAAAH!

Acknowledgements

My thanks to the following: the great students I've met along the way; the adults who remember what it's like to be a child; my publisher; and the horribly delicious O. Penn-Coughin family.

About the Author

At last count, O. Penn-Coughin has visited hundreds of schools in recent years, sharing his twisted tales with more than 100,000 students. When not on the road, he *haunts* Bend, Oregon with his wife, two daughters, and one scary cat.

Learn more at **CoughinBooks.com** and listen to O. Penn-Coughin read his stories on **The Scary Story Podcast**.

Made in the USA
Columbia, SC
10 November 2017